P9-CQD-112

This book belongs to

_____

Published by Advance Publishers

© 1998 Disney Enterprises, Inc.

All rights reserved. Printed in the United States.

No part of this book may be reproduced or copied in any form
without the written permission of the copyright owner.

Written by Lisa Ann Marsoli
Illustrated by Phil Ortiz, Dean Kleven, and Diana Wakeman
Produced by Bumpy Slide Books

ISBN: 1-885222-97-1

10 9 8 7 6 5 4 3 2 1

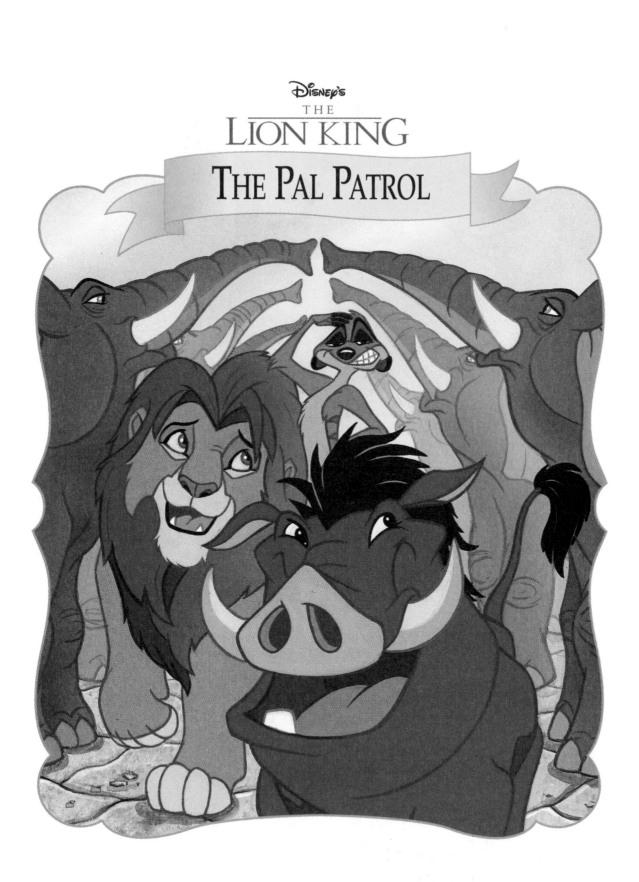

Timon and Pumbaa waited . . . and waited . . . and waited. They were supposed to meet Simba at Pride Rock over an hour ago, and he still wasn't there.

"What did I tell you?" Timon complained to Pumbaa. "A guy becomes king and suddenly he forgets about the little people. The ones who knew him when he was all alone with no one to turn to."

"I heard that!" called Simba as he came up behind his buddies. "And I didn't forget you. There was an emergency. A whole elephant herd slipped on some banana peels. Why can't those monkeys remember to clean up after themselves?!"

Pumbaa looked confused. "I thought monkeys never forgot," he said.

"That's elephants," answered Timon, rolling his eyes. "*Elephants* never forget."

The three pals headed off to enjoy a lazy day in the Pride Lands.

"Ahhh, together again — finally!" said Timon.

"Yeah," agreed Simba. "Hakuna matata. No worries! At least for one afternoon."

Lately Simba just didn't seem to have as much time to spend with his old friends. Being the Lion King meant that Simba was always needed for something.

"Oh, Simba! Oh, Simba!" Zazu's voice came drifting up from behind them. "Come quick! One of the cubs has its head stuck in a tree again!"

Then the cranky hornbill turned to Timon and Pumbaa. "It's all your fault," he declared. "Teaching the cubs how to hunt for bugs. Disgraceful behavior! Simply disgraceful!"

"What's eating him?" asked Pumbaa.

"Nothing," answered Timon. "He's too tough and gamy!"

Simba laughed. "Very funny. But seriously, guys, I'm sorry. I've got to go, but I'll catch up with you later."

"Simba," asked Pumbaa, "do you like being the Lion King? I mean, isn't it an awful lot of responsibility?"

"Well, sure," answered his friend. "But I like having everyone depend on me to keep them safe. It makes me feel as if I'm doing something that matters."

As Pumbaa and Timon watched Simba head off with Zazu, Timon shook his head. "Just listen to him," said Timon in disgust. "Is he a bore or what?"

Pumbaa looked confused. "I thought I was the boar," he said.

Timon gave his pal a playful tap. "Oh, well," said Timon. "At least we don't have any responsibilities to tie us down. Let's go have some fun. Whaddaya say?"

"I say, 'hakuna matata,'" Pumbaa replied.

"Exactly!" agreed Timon.

And so the two wandered off into the brush, looking for grubs — and whatever adventure might come their way.

Soon Pumbaa's stomach started to rumble, so he and Timon stopped to rustle up some grubs for lunch.

While Pumbaa rooted around under a rock,

Timon stuck his head in a tree the way he had taught the cubs to do.

"Boy, Timon! It sure is hot!" Pumbaa called. "I'm sweatin' like a pig!"

Timon emerged from the tree with a leaf full of colorful insects. "You ain't kiddin'," he told Pumbaa. "I'm on fire!"

The warthog looked up from his bug hunting. "Yikes!" he cried, his eyes opening wide. "If we don't watch it, we both will be!"

Timon whirled around and saw that the grass just behind them was on fire. Right now the flames were small, but with all the dried brush around them, Timon knew the fire could grow fierce in no time.

"Let's go get Simba!" shouted Pumbaa. "He'll know what to do!"

"There's no time for that," Timon declared. "It's up to us. Got any ideas?"

"I know!" Pumbaa exclaimed. "How about I stay here and keep everyone away while you go to the water hole?"

"I don't have time for a dip, Pumbaa. This is serious!" Timon yelled.

"No, I meant maybe there will be someone there who can help us," Pumbaa explained.

So Timon ran to the water hole as fast as he could while Pumbaa posted himself as guard near the fire.

"Don't worry!" Timon called over his shoulder.
"Everything's gonna be all right!" But he wasn't
so sure.

Pumbaa paced, nervously glancing back at the fire every few seconds. Soon, in the distance, he could make out some shapes moving quickly toward him.

"That must be Timon back with help already! What a relief!" he sighed. But as the shapes got closer, he saw that it wasn't Timon at all. It was a herd of zebras on the move.

Pumbaa ran toward them, whooping as loudly as he could. But they didn't seem to see him. "Hey! Stop!" he screamed as the herd thundered closer.

Then, just as Pumbaa closed his eyes, expecting the worst, the animals came to an abrupt halt.

Pumbaa let out a sigh of relief and explained
to the zebras about the fire. The leader of the herd
was grateful, and quickly led the animals away
from the blaze.

As Pumbaa watched the babies tagging along after their mothers, he felt happy knowing he had kept them out of danger.

Moments later, Timon did arrive — and he was followed by a long line of elephants. "Did I strike it big or what?" Timon called, gesturing toward his pachyderm parade. "Pumbaa, meet the fire brigade!"

While Timon yelled out directions, the elephants sprayed the fire with water from their trunks. "That's the way! Just a little more and this fire will be history!" Timon told them.

A small elephant approached and blasted Timon
with his trunk. "You gotta work on your aim, kid,"
said Timon, shaking the water from his body.

By the time Simba arrived, all that remained of the blaze were delicate wisps of smoke curling into the afternoon sky.

"I came as soon as the zebras told me," said Simba, "but it looks like you two handled things on your own."

Pumbaa looked proud, while Timon acted embarrassed.

"Aw, go on! It was nothin', really. So we saved the Pride Lands — it's all in a day's work for me and Pumbaa here," Timon explained.

A slow smile spread across Simba's face.
"Hmmm. A day's work . . . that gives me an idea,"
he said.

"Since you guys get around so much," Simba suggested, "how would you like to be the official fire patrol of the Pride Lands? That is, if it wouldn't be too much responsibility."

"Okay, here's the deal," Timon replied. "If we're going to start acting responsible, you're gonna have to lighten up a little. Stop and smell the stinkbugs, for Pete's sake! Deal?"

"Deal," Simba agreed, bounding off into the distance. "Last one to the water hole's a rotten ostrich egg!"

"Look who's all fired up now!" wisecracked Timon, climbing up on Pumbaa's back.

"Ahh, just like the old days," Pumbaa said cheerfully as he took off running after their pal, the Lion King.

Pumbaa and Timon
Thought that Simba was no fun,
'Cause since their pal became a king
His work was never done.
Then they found out for themselves
How good it feels inside
To have a job to call your own,
One you can do with pride.